D0306968

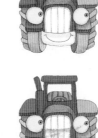

CONTENTS

First Published 2005 by Brown Watson
The Old Mill, 76 Fleckney Road,
Kibworth Beauchamp, Leics LE8 0HG

ISBN: 978-0-7097-1653-2

© 2005 Brown Watson, England
Reprinted 2006 (twice), 2007, 2009, 2010, 2012

Printed in China

Now I Can
READ
15 Drive Along Tales

Stories by Maureen Spurgeon
Illustrations by Gill Guile

Brown Watson
ENGLAND

TUBBY AND SPEEDY

Tubby the Tractor did not go very fast. Speedy the Sports Car was always teasing him.

'Hoot! Hoot!' he hooted, speeding down the lane. 'See how I race along!'

'Stop!' cried Farmer Bell. 'You have made my chickens run off!'

'You have scared the sheep!' said Tubby. But Speedy did not care.

It began to rain. For the rest of the day and all night, it rained hard. Next day Tubby had to go even slower across the muddy ground.

'Poor old Tubby!' hooted Speedy. 'I can go fast, rain or no rain!' SPLASH! Speedy went right into a big puddle, drenching the sheep in muddy water! 'Hoot! Hoot!' hooted Speedy. 'Hoot! Hoot!'

The rain had made the lane very wet and VERY slippery. Speedy was going much too fast...

'HOOT!' Now, Speedy was slipping and skidding. He tried to slow down. He tried to stop.

'Look out!' shouted Farmer Bell. 'The pond!' But it was too late.

SPLASH! Now, Speedy was drenched in water!

'Come on, Tubby,' said Farmer Bell. He drove him to the edge of the pond. Then he tied one end of a rope to Tubby's tow bar and the other end to Speedy's bumper.

'Now!' said Farmer Bell. 'Pull!' Tubby did enjoy pulling Speedy out of the pond! Towing him back down the lane was even more fun!

'Hoot! Hoot!' went Tubby the Tractor. 'Now I am going MUCH faster than you, Speedy!'

READ THESE WORDS AGAIN!

teasing   hooted

speeding   chickens

scared   sheep

rained   slower

muddy   ground

splash   puddle

drenching   slippery

tried   enjoy

WHAT CAN YOU SEE HERE?

tractor

farmer

sports car

tow bar

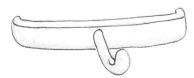

pond

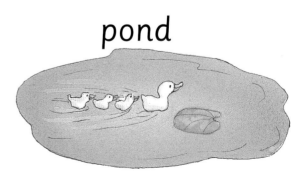

HERE COMES JESSIE!

All the animals at the big safari park knew Jessie the Jeep! She was always busy, bringing things for them or taking Wendy, her driver, around the safari park.

One day, Wendy drove the vet to see a monkey and her baby.

'The baby is still small,' said the vet. 'But she is doing well!'

'Good!' said the keeper. 'It is the first baby for that monkey!'

'Come on, Jessie!' smiled Wendy. 'You can see Baby Monkey later!'

Jessie fetched hay and blankets for the donkeys. She worked hard all day. Then Wendy got a call on her radio.

'Baby Monkey is missing!' cried the keeper. 'Have you seen her?'

'No!' said Wendy. 'I shall drive around the safari park in Jessie!'

'Good idea!' said the keeper. 'The monkey is fretting badly! And the baby needs her mother!'

They looked all over the safari park.

'It will be dark soon!' said Wendy. 'We must find her!'

'We are all worried!' said the keeper. 'Only Jessie doesn't seem upset!'

'I feel cold!' said Wendy. 'I left my jacket on the back seat!'

She reached across – and touched something furry! It was Baby Monkey, fast asleep!

'Well!' said Wendy. 'Thanks, Jessie!'

Baby Monkey liked riding in Jessie! And when she saw her baby, Mother Monkey jumped up on the jeep!

'Look at that!' said Wendy. 'ALL the animals DO know Jessie the Jeep!'

READ THESE WORDS AGAIN!

knew	animals
busy	driver
around	baby
small	later
fetched	blankets
idea	worried
jacket	know

WHAT CAN YOU SEE HERE?

vet

jeep

safari park

donkeys

monkeys

FIRE ENGINE FRED

Fire Engine Fred was at the Town Show. 'Can I work the hose?' asked a boy.

'There is no fire!' said Fireman Tim. 'You can sound the bell instead!'

CLANG-CLANG! The boy enjoyed ringing Fred's bell! But Fred DID wish that there WAS a fire to put out!

All the way back to the fire station, Fred kept thinking about putting out a real fire. Then he saw a tall swirl of black smoke...

'Fire!' shouted Fireman Bill, clanging the bell. 'There is a fire at Betty Baker's cottage!'

Fred raced to the cottage.

'Get the hose, Bill!' said Tim. 'Fix it to the water-tap and aim it at the window! I am going inside!'

There was smoke inside the cottage!

'Betty!' cried Tim. 'Let me carry you into the garden, away from the fire!'

'There is NO fire!' cried Betty. 'I burnt some bread, so I opened the window to let the smoke out!'

Poor Tim! 'We have soaked your kitchen with water from Fred's hose!' he said. 'I am so sorry.'

Betty smiled. 'Fred is enjoying the sunshine!' she said. 'Bring my things out here to dry and then we can do the same! We can all have some of the cakes I have baked!'

'We are glad you did not have a real fire!' said Bill.

'So am I!' said Betty. 'And it is good to know that you and Fire Engine Fred are always ready to help when people need you!'

READ THESE WORDS AGAIN!

asked	sound
instead	clang
enjoyed	swirl
smoke	cottage
raced	cakes
opened	kitchen
sorry	people

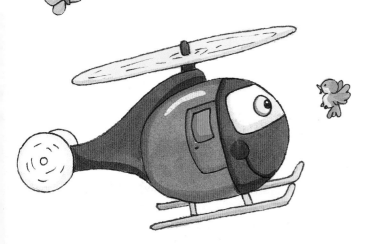

WHAT CAN YOU SEE HERE?

hose

fire station

fireman

long ladder

fire engine

A NEW JOB FOR VICTOR

Victor the Van did all sorts of jobs for Greg's grocery store. He liked it best of all when Greg took grocery orders to the customers who lived out of town.

'Your groceries, Doctor Pott!' said Greg. 'Must dash, Miss Todd wants food for her cats! Then off we go to see old Mister Wells!'

Everybody said that Greg and Victor did a good job. It was just a shame that Greg's grocery store was not a bit nearer…

Then Greg was told that the store had to be pulled down to make way for a new road.

'Do not worry!' Greg told his customers. 'This is not the end for me and Victor!'

Poor Victor! First, Greg sawed a big hole in his bodywork!

'This will be the window!' said Greg.

He fitted new shelves and racks, then they went to the big warehouse.

Soon, Victor was loaded up with tins of beans, jars of jam, packets of coffee and lots more!

'Are you opening a new store, Greg?' asked the warehouse man.

'Yes!' said Greg. 'Greg's Mobile Store! Victor is the store! Come on, Victor, we are on our way!'

Doctor Pott was glad to see Greg and Victor! So were all the people who lived nearby!

'It is good to see you, Greg,' said Miss Todd. 'I cannot carry heavy shopping back from town!'

'No problem!' said Greg. 'Victor and I, we can bring you all the things you need!'

READ THESE WORDS AGAIN!

grocery	store
orders	liked
lived	off
everybody	shame
loaded	heavy
worry	racks
shopping	problem
shelves	bodywork

WHAT CAN YOU SEE HERE?

customers

groceries

mobile store

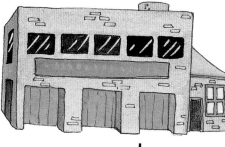

warehouse

packets

AMY THE AMBULANCE

'Calling Amy the Ambulance! Susan Mills has had a fall in Hill Park. Bring her to hospital! Over!'

Jo, Amy's driver, flicked a switch on her radio. 'Amy calling! We are on our way! Over and out!'

Susan was crying. 'My arm hurts! And my doll is broken!'

'It is her arm that is broken!' said Nurse Paula. 'Amy the Ambulance will take you both to hospital!'

'I do not want to go to hospital!' sobbed Susan.

'Dina cannot go alone,' said Mum.

Susan gave a sniff. She stopped crying. 'All right,' she said.

Paula helped Susan into Amy the Ambulance. 'Dina needs a plaster on her face,' she said. 'Let us find one in Amy's first-aid box!' Susan put a plaster on Dina's face. Then she helped to bandage Dina's leg.

At the hospital, a doctor took an X-ray picture of Susan's arm. 'You have broken your arm,' he said. 'We must put it in a plaster cast. It will mend in six weeks.'

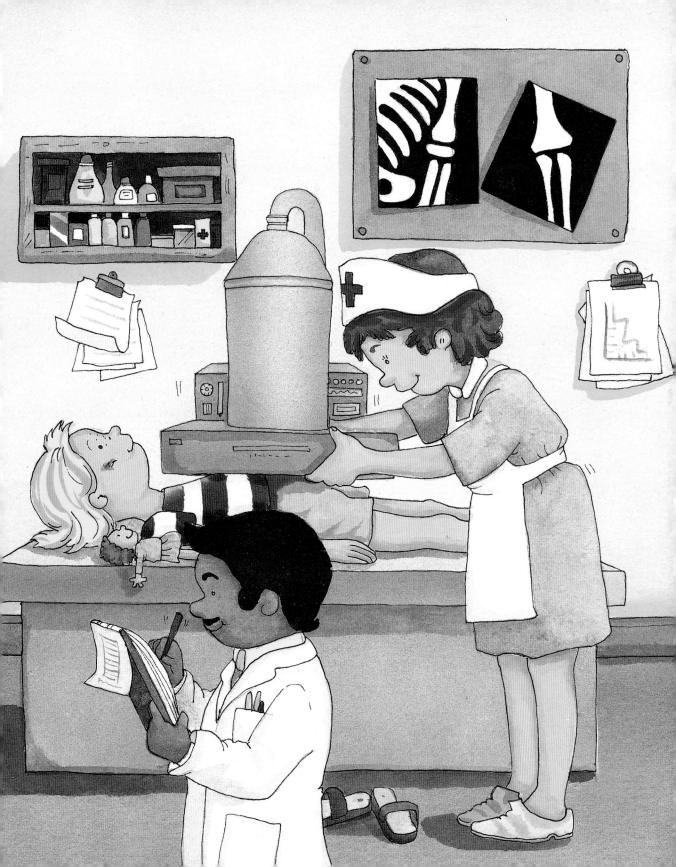

Later, Paula put Dina's broken arm in plaster, too. 'Dina's plaster cannot come off,' said Mum. 'Toys cannot mend like we can, Susan.'

Susan stroked Dina's hair. 'I do not think she minds,' she said, 'as long as she can stay with Amy!'

'Good idea!' said Paula. 'With her big smile, her arm in a sling and a plaster on her face, she will make everyone feel better about going to hospital!'

'Yes!' said Susan. 'And Amy the Ambulance will be taking them!'

READ THESE WORDS AGAIN!

driver   flicked

switch   radio

crying   broken

nurse   hospital

sobbed   plaster

bandage   cannot

stroked   everyone

WHAT CAN YOU SEE HERE?

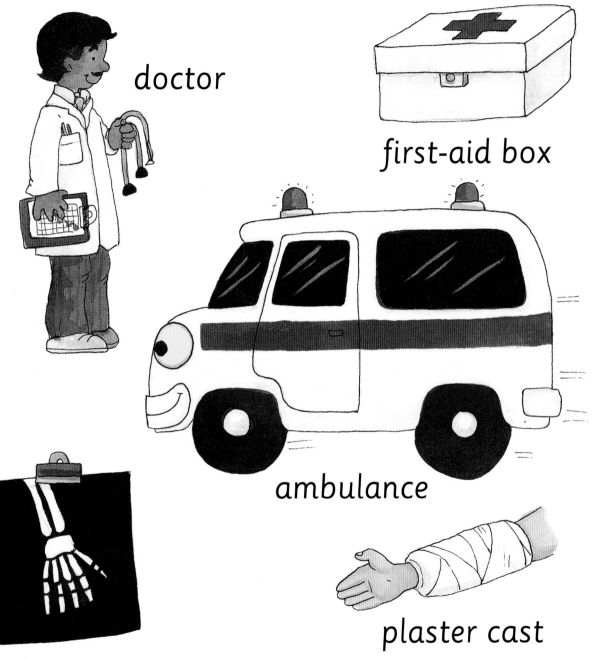

doctor

first-aid box

ambulance

X-ray picture

plaster cast

45

CLARA, AT HOME AND AWAY

To Todd and Una, Clara the Caravan was a friend. With Clara being towed by the family car, they went to stay at the seaside, in camping parks, forests and woods.

'I like going to bed in Clara's pull-down bunks!' said Todd.

'I like keeping all our toys in Clara's lockers,' said Una.

'But it will soon be time for us to go back to school,' said Todd.

'We will miss being in Clara,' said Una. They felt sad about that.

'Cheer up!' said Mum. 'Clara will be taking us to Uncle Tony's wedding this weekend!'

Uncle Tony lived in an apartment block. In the grounds was a big garden. And in the garden was a marquee, like a big tent.

'This is for our wedding party!' said Uncle Tony. 'You can put Clara here!'

It was a nice wedding. But being with Clara made it even nicer.

'I DO like your caravan!' said Sally, Uncle Tony's wife. 'It must be such fun, staying inside!'

'Come and see us!' said Mum. 'Then you can stay in Clara, too!'

'Can we stay in Clara?' asked Una. 'When we go home, I mean?'

'That is a good idea!' said Mum.

So when she is not taking them on trips to the seaside, forests or camping parks, Clara is a playroom for Una and Todd, where they can invite friends. And there is always room for visitors!

'Being with Clara is as much fun at home as when we go away!' said Todd. 'She is a real friend!'

READ THESE WORDS AGAIN!

friend	towed
family	lockers
school	uncle
grounds	wedding
party	nicer
inside	idea
invite	visitors

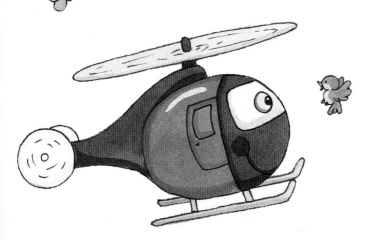

WHAT CAN YOU SEE HERE?

caravan

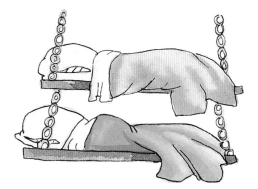

pull-down bunks

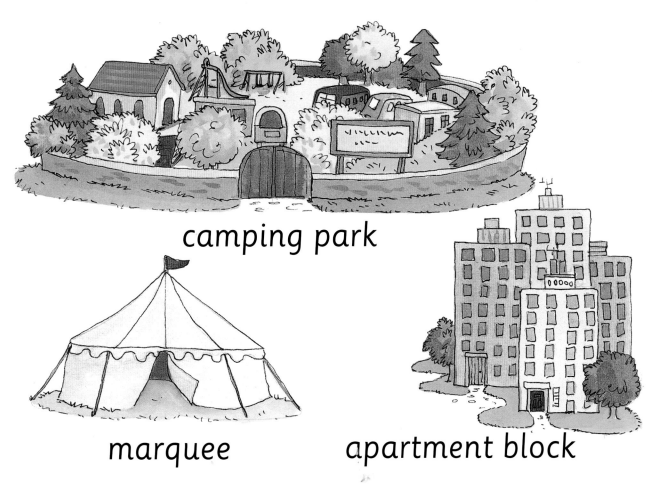

camping park

marquee

apartment block

TAMMY'S SURPRISE FARE

'Taxi!' Tammy the Taxi was always busy!

'I hope we do not have to go far,' said Ted, her driver. 'I want to see a football match on television!'

'Taxi!' a man cried. 'Will you take me to the railway station?'

'Certainly!' said Ted. They soon got there. Then, as the man paid his fare, there came the cry, 'Taxi!'

It was a lady with lots of luggage.

'Can you take me to the airport?' she asked.

'Certainly,' said Ted. The airport was further away. When they got there, someone else cried, 'Taxi!'

'Please take us to the Town Hotel!' It was a man with his wife and children.

'Certainly!' said Ted. They had hardly reached the hotel when someone else cried 'Taxi!'

'A waitress has had a fall!' said a porter. 'Please, take her to hospital!'

The hospital was even further away. But Tammy hoped Ted might get home in time to see the football match.

'Taxi!' This time, it was the Mayor. 'I have been visiting the hospital and it is nearly time for my next appointment. Can I go in your taxi?'

'Certainly,' said Ted, further from home than ever. 'Where to, sir?'

'North End football stadium!' said the mayor. 'There is a match tonight! Why not come and see the game with me? That is, if you are not doing anything else!'

'Thanks,' grinned Ted. 'Tammy the Taxi and I, we were only going home to watch television!'

READ THESE WORDS AGAIN!

match	railway
station	fare
asked	further
cried	hotel
children	porter
waitress	hoped
visiting	appointment

WHAT CAN YOU SEE HERE?

television

luggage

taxi

mayor

football stadium

WE LOVE HATTIE!

Hattie the Helicopter was landing at a big airport. 'Steady, Hattie,' said Roy, her pilot.

'We have fetched roses from Star Island!' Roy told a lady officer.

'Just in time for the visit by the Group Captain!' said the lady. 'Please stay and have a rest!'

'I never rest!' snorted a jumbo jet. 'And I fly around the world!'

'I have rescued people at sea,' said Hattie. 'And I have landed in the jungle!'

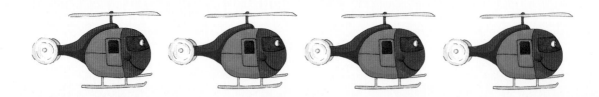

'Sssh!' came a voice. 'Here is the Group Captain!'

The Captain looked splendid in his uniform. 'Star Island roses!' he said. 'Look, Posy and Tim!'

'Oh, Grandpa,' said Tim. 'We wanted to go up in an aeroplane!'

'But these aircraft need a lot of fuel to make them go,' said the Captain. 'And they need lots of space to take off.' Then he saw Hattie. 'A helicopter!' he said. 'Now, that needs no space at all to take off. What about fuel, pilot?'

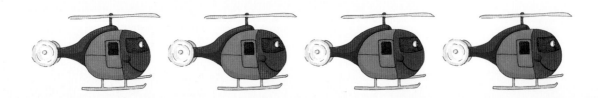

'Plenty in the tank, sir!' said Roy.

'Then let's go!' said the Captain. They got inside. Hattie's rotor blades whirred, taking them up into the sky.

'There is Star Island!' said the Captain. 'Steady, Hattie!'

Roy flew Hattie all around Star Island before landing back at the airport. 'That was great, Grandpa!' said Tim. 'Thank you!'

'You must thank Hattie!' said the Captain. 'She made it happen!'

'Yes!' said Posy. 'We LOVE Hattie the Helicopter!'

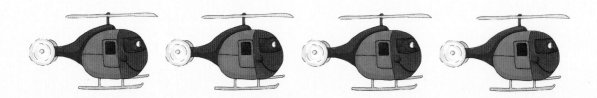

READ THESE WORDS AGAIN!

pilot   star

island   officer

visit   snorted

world   rescued

people   uniform

aeroplane   fuel

whirred   happen

WHAT CAN YOU SEE HERE?

Captain

rotor blades

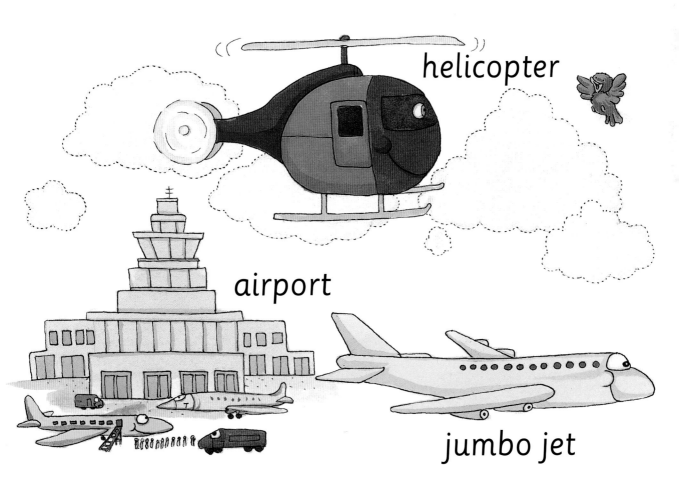

helicopter

airport

jumbo jet

MITCH, THE MAILVAN

Mitch the Mailvan had almost finished work. When the day began, he had been loaded up with letters, cards, parcels and packets. Now, there was one parcel left.

'Who is this for, Mitch?' asked Dave. 'The label is torn. I can only read Mi... I know! It must be for Miss Dixon, the baker!'

But the parcel was not for Miss Dixon. 'So, who is it for?' said Dave. 'I can only read Mi...'

'I think I know!' said Miss Dixon.

And off she went without another word.

'Mi..' read Dave again. 'Who is this for, Mitch? I know! It must be Mike Bond at the garage!'

But the parcel was not for Mike.

'So, who is it for?' said Dave. 'Look! I can just make out Mi...'

'I think I know!' said Mike. And off he went without another word.

'Mi..' said Dave, trying to read the label again. 'Who is this for, Mitch? I know! It must be Mill Lane School!'

But the parcel was not for Mill Lane School.

'So, who is it for?' said Dave.

Then, Mitch saw Miss Dixon and Mike Bond, together with all the children at Mill Lane School.

'Open it!' they shouted all together. 'Open the parcel!'

So, Dave opened the parcel. And inside was a shiny new name-plate with the name 'MITCH' on it.

'Well, well!' smiled Dave. 'Now, we know who the parcel was for!'

READ THESE WORDS AGAIN!

almost   finished
loaded   letters
cards   packets
who   only
think   know
another   word
garage   school
together   open

WHAT CAN YOU SEE HERE?

parcel

label

mailvan

name-plate

children

MINNIE AND MILLY

Ken drove Minnie the Minibus. They knew all the passengers, except one. She was an old lady who got on the bus each morning. She hardly spoke. She never smiled. Nobody even knew her name.

One day, as Minnie waited for the old lady, in jumped a little dog!

Tim Holt looked at the dog's collar.

'Look, John!' he said to his friend. 'Her name is Milly!'

'And there is an address,' said John. '10, Cherry Road.'

'I know where that is!' said Ken. 'Milly can come with us to town. Then we can take her back home.'

'Woof!' barked Milly. Everyone began to pat and stroke her, and all the time she was wagging her tail.

'All change!' cried Ken at the last stop. 'Time for a walk, Milly!'

Minnie felt sad when the time came to go back. It had been nice to have Milly on board and everyone talking about her.

'This your stop, Milly!' said Ken. 'WOOF!' barked Milly.

'Milly!' cried a voice. 'Why did you run off?' It was the old lady.

'Woof!' barked Milly, her tail wagging again. 'Woof-woof!'

'She had your address on the disc on her collar,' explained Ken. 'Miss.. er'

'You can call me Dolly,' smiled the lady. 'I have not had Milly long. She is all I have to stop me from being lonely.'

'Well, now you know everyone on Minnie the Minibus,' said Ken. 'Thanks to Milly!'

'Woof!' barked Milly.

READ THESE WORDS AGAIN!

drove   except

morning   nobody

knew   jumped

friend   address

everyone   change

board   barked

lonely   know

WHAT CAN YOU SEE HERE?

passengers

disc

minibus

collar

old lady

NO LEAVES ON THE LINE!

Eddie liked being a steam engine, even though he only pulled trucks on a goods line. Dennis the Diesel pulled the trains on the main line.

'How slow you are!' he snorted at Eddie. 'Still, you only pull trucks!'

'I am as good as you are!' Eddie puffed. But Dennis whizzed past.

The days began to get shorter. The leaves were beginning to fall.

'More coal in your fire-box, Eddie!' said Dave, his driver. 'We need lots of steam today!'

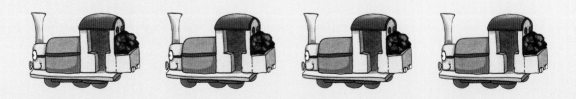

'Coal!' cried Dennis. 'Steam! Hah!'

Eddie was just getting up steam, when there was a loud screech.

'Sounds like Dennis is in trouble on the main line!' said Dave. 'And just listen to those passengers!'

The passengers were very cross!

'Why has the train stopped?'

'What is wrong with the engine?'

'Fallen leaves are clogging up the line!' said the driver. 'The engine cannot move!'

A man pointed at Eddie. 'That engine is moving!' he said.

'The sparks from Eddie's fire-box burn up leaves as soon as they fall!' said Dave. 'Leaves on the line are no problem for us!'

'Then Eddie can pull our train!' said an important-looking man. 'I am a director of the railway!'

So Dennis was shunted away and Eddie puffed down the line, burning all the leaves as he went.

'Hurrah!' cried the passengers.

'Hurrah!' puffed Eddie.

And if Dennis did say anything, nobody heard him.

READ THESE WORDS AGAIN!

leaves	pulled
trains	main
snorted	whizzed
shorter	screech
trouble	wrong
clogging	heard
important	director
burning	move

WHAT CAN YOU SEE HERE?

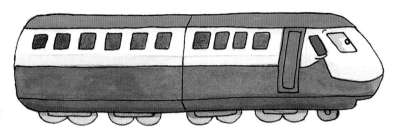

diesel engine

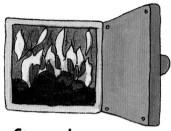

fire-box

passengers

steam engine

driver

MONTY ON THE MOVE

Monty had been a fine motorbike, crowds cheering as he raced around the track. 'Good old Monty!' 'Monty wins!'

Then came the day when his wheels stopped turning. 'No more races, Monty,' said Keith, his rider. 'You are going to a theme park!'

At the theme park there was a little railway, a boating lake, model cars… and a museum.

'This is your new home, Monty!' said Keith. 'In you go!'

But how Monty hated the idea of just standing still, getting rusty!

'Hey!' came a voice. 'Look at that motorbike!' A boy got into the saddle and gripped Monty's handlebars. 'Brrm, brrm!' he said.

'Get off, Max!' said the boy's dad. But other children wanted to climb up on Monty, too!

'Brrm, brrm! Brrm, brrm!' 'My turn next!' 'Good old Monty!'

Then two mechanics came and wheeled Monty away. 'This bike is just what we needed!' one said.

Monty did not hear them. He was dreaming that he was a fine motor-bike once more, crowds cheering. 'Good old Monty!' 'Monty wins!'

Hands gripped his handlebars. Someone was sitting in his saddle, and then – 'Brrm, brrm!'

'Look at me on the motorbike!' someone shouted. 'He is the best thing on this roundabout. Hurrah!'

'Better than him standing still and getting rusty!' said the mechanics.

Now, Monty is on the move all day long! Brrm, brrm!

READ THESE WORDS AGAIN!

crowds	cheering
raced	track
hurrah	wheels
railway	boating
museum	idea
gripped	saddle
better	move

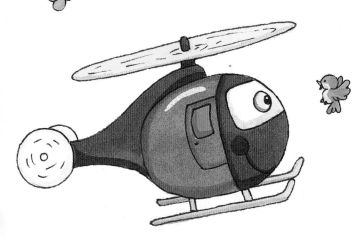

WHAT CAN YOU SEE HERE?

motorbike

handlebars

theme park

roundabout

mechanics

BOB'S HEAVY LOAD

'My truck has broken down!' said Tina, the potter. 'It is loaded up!'

'Bob the Breakdown Van will tow it back to your studio,' said Al. 'You can unload your things and leave it outside. We will tow it to my garage tomorrow.'

It was hard work pulling Tina's truck with such a heavy load. Bob looked forward to it being empty!

Next day, a man came with some clay for Tina. 'I will put this in her truck,' he said to himself.

Bob did not know about the clay. He only knew the truck felt heavy!

Al put on the brakes. As Bob stopped, apples fell from a tree and into Tina's truck! Now, Bob's load felt even heavier!

Men were cutting logs. 'More odd branches, Pete!' one shouted. He threw them across and they landed in Tina's truck!

'Where do you want these sacks, Mack?' said Pete.

'In the truck!' cried Mack. But Pete threw them into Tina's truck!

By now, Bob's load was so heavy, he was glad to get to Al's garage.

'See what was in Tina's truck!' said Al. 'Clay, apples, bundles of branches and a pile of sacks. Sacks are just what we need!'

'Apples!' cried Al's son, Jay. 'And I need branches for my wigwam!'

'I need that clay!' came Tina's voice. 'The man from the clay-works said it was in my truck!'

'And apples, branches and sacks!' said Jay. 'And Bob the Breakdown Van pulled the whole load!'

READ THESE WORDS AGAIN!

truck	broken
loaded	leave
outside	garage
tomorrow	work
forward	empty
clay	apples
heavier	whole
logs	threw

WHAT CAN YOU SEE HERE?

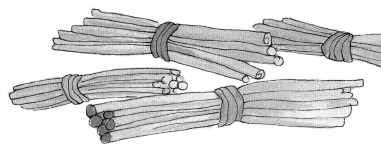

potter

studio

breakdown van

bundles of branches

wigwam

IDA IS ON HER WAY!

Ding-dong! Ding-dong! Everyone liked seeing Ida the Ice-Cream Van on a hot summer's day. Ice-cream cones, milkshakes, choc ices... her customers liked them all.

'It has been a busy summer,' said Rob as he drove Ida home.

'Yes,' agreed his girlfriend, Rosie. 'But Ida will not have many customers when winter comes.'

What Rosie said was true. On cold days, nobody came to buy ice creams, milkshakes or choc ices.

One day, Rob pushed Ida out into the road. 'Cleaning time, Ida!' he said. 'Then we'll cover you up so you can keep warm all winter.'

'I do not want that!' Ida said to herself. 'I want to be out on the road, seeing all my customers!'

Then, just as Rob was polishing Ida's headlamps, along came a lorry.

'Hi!' called the driver. 'Any idea where I can get something to eat for myself and my mate?'

'No,' said Rosie. 'But I can put some tea into a flask for you.'

'And I can heat up some sausage rolls!' said Rob.

'Thanks!' said the driver. 'We have been looking for somewhere to eat for hours! Seeing your smart van made us stop and ask!'

So, Rosie went to make the tea and Rob went to heat up some sausage rolls to put in a bag. And they both had the same idea...

Ding-dong! Ding-dong! Now, everyone likes seeing Ida on a winter's day! Hot drinks, pies, rolls, burgers...customers like them all!

READ THESE WORDS AGAIN!

everyone   summer
girlfriend   cleaning
cover   winter
polishing   herself
called   idea
something   myself
mate   somewhere
burgers   ask

WHAT CAN YOU SEE HERE?

milkshake

customers

ice-cream van

flask

sausage roll

DON AND BIGGER DIGGER

Don the Digger had come to dig a sandpit at Barn School.

'Huh!' snorted Bigger Digger. 'A sandpit! I will be digging a road!'

'Our school is where Farmer Day's family home used to be,' Miss Foot was saying.

'And I do wish I was able to show you what it was like when I was a boy!' said Farmer Day.

Don went on digging. Then – CLANG!

'Hah!' said Bigger Digger. 'You are in trouble now!'

'Don hit an old, tin trunk,' said his driver. 'It was under the ground!'

'Grandad's trunk!' said Farmer Day. 'So that is where it was!'

Don scooped out the trunk. It was damp and rusty, but Farmer Day managed to lift the lid. So many things were inside!

'Grandma's milking stool!' cried Farmer Day. 'And the yoke she used to carry the pails of milk! Grandad's wind-up gramophone! And all these pictures!'

And that was not all.

There were toys and games, hoops and sticks, even some clothes!

'I want Barn School to have these things,' said Farmer Day. 'I wanted you to see how things used to be. Now I have my wish.'

'So, Don grants wishes!' said his driver. The children cheered.

'Don found the tin trunk!' said Miss Foot, happily.

'Don is a GREAT digger!' cried Farmer Day.

And Bigger Digger? He said nothing at all.

READ THESE WORDS AGAIN!

school   bigger

trouble   under

ground   scooped

pictures   hoops

sticks   clothes

wanted   grants

nothing   wishes

WHAT CAN YOU SEE HERE?

wind-up gramophone

yoke

digger

tin trunk

milking stool